IN THE
Red Canoe

WRITTEN BY

Leslie A. Davidson

ILLUSTRATED BY

Laura Bifano

ORCA BOOK PUBLISHERS

I like to go in the red canoe,

I sit low in the bow.

I can paddle by myself

my Grandpa taught me how.

We don't say much—we mostly look.
He shows me everything.
The watery world goes sliding by.
Our paddles dip and swing.

He points out trees that beavers chew,
he knows just where they go.
Their lodges heaped up by the shore
with tunnels deep below.

Swimming 'round the red canoe
are schools of fishy fry.
Grandpa holds me while I lean
to catch them flashing by.

We paddle up to baby ducks
who quickly turn around.
They motorboat their little legs
and make a splashy sound.

Green lily pads like floating hearts
hold yellow flowers up.
And dragonflies with shining wings
rest on these petal cups.

We find a place to hunt for frogs,
a secret, muddy beach.
How do they always know to stay
just one hop out of reach?

An osprey's wings beat like a fan.
She circles, then she stops.
Grandpa and I, we hold our breath
when, in a flash, she drops.

Her mighty talons grip a fish.
We laugh to see her rise.
Water droplets, soaring bird
and slippery, silver prize.

Sunset time is swallow hour,
we drift along the shore.
First one, then two, swoop overhead.
Then more, and more, and more!

I love to watch the swallows dance,
my head on Grandpa's knee.
In my dreams I fly with them—
do swallows dream of me?

Sometimes we paddle in the dark
on still and starlit nights.
A lantern sits upon the bow,
the lake a million lights.

Gentle waves, a loon's wild call,
we rock and dream and float.
I shiver right down to my bones—
there's magic near our boat.

I wish upon the shining moon
that there will always be
Grandpa and the red canoe,
soft summer nights...

and me.

For Lincoln
—L.D.

To my husband Caleb, my family, and my friends.
You guys all encouraged and supported me through the
creation of this book and I'd be a hot mess without you.
—L.B.

Cataloguing in Publication information available from Library and Archives Canada
ISBN 978-1-4598-0973-4 (hardback)

First published in the United States, 2016
Library of Congress Control Number: 2016931886

Summary: In this rhyming picture book, a young girl describes the magical encounters
with wildlife that she and her grandfather witness while out in the red canoe.

Orca Book Publishers is dedicated to preserving the environment and has printed
this book on Forest Stewardship Council® certified paper.

Orca Book Publishers gratefully acknowledges the support for its publishing programs provided
by the following agencies: the Government of Canada through the Canada Book Fund
and the Canada Council for the Arts, and the Province of British Columbia
through the BC Arts Council and the Book Publishing Tax Credit.

Artwork created using gouache on paper.

Cover and interior artwork by Laura Bifano
Design by Teresa Bubela

ORCA BOOK PUBLISHERS
www.orcabook.com

Printed and bound in Canada.

19 18 17 16 • 5 4 3 2